Farmer Finn's
Silly Sheep

by Damian Harvey and
Steve Brown

W
FRANKLIN WATTS
LONDON•SYDNEY

Franklin Watts

First published in Great Britain in 2016 by
The Watts Publishing Group

Text © Damian Harvey 2016
Illustrations © Steve Brown 2016

The rights of Damian Harvey to be identified as the
author and Steve Brown as the illustrator of this Work
have been asserted in accordance with the Copyright, Designs
and Patents Act, 1988.

Series Editor: Jackie Hamley
Series Advisor: Catherine Glavina
Series Designer: Peter Scoulding

A CIP catalogue record for this book is available
from the British Library.

ISBN 978 1 4451 4574 7 (hbk)
ISBN 978 1 4451 4576 1 (pbk)
ISBN 978 1 4451 4575 4 (library ebook)

Printed in China

FSC
www.fsc.org
MIX
Paper from
responsible sources
FSC® C104740

Franklin Watts
An imprint of
Hachette Children's Group
Part of The Watts Publishing Group
Carmelite House
50 Victoria Embankment
London EC4Y 0DZ

An Hachette UK company.
www.hachette.co.uk

www.franklinwatts.co.uk

It was a wet and windy morning. "What a horrible day!" said Farmer Finn.

He put on his woolly hat,
zipped up his coat,

Grandad is
No 1

and stepped into
his boots.

First, Finn fed the hens in
the henhouse.

Then he milked the cows.

"Now for the sheep," said Finn.

But halfway across the farmyard, he stopped.

The barn door was
wide open.

"Oh no!" cried Farmer
Finn. "Those silly sheep."

11

There were no sheep in the barn.

"Perhaps they're in the orchard," said Finn.

But there were no sheep to be found and Finn lost his hat.

"Where *are* those silly sheep?"

"Perhaps they're up the hill," said Finn.

But there were no sheep to be found and Finn lost his coat.

"Where *are* those silly sheep?"

Finn could not find the
sheep anywhere.

Then he lost his boots in all the mud.

"That's it!" said Farmer Finn.

"I'm going home where it's nice and warm."

But halfway across the farmyard, he stopped.

The farmhouse door was wide open.

"Oh no!" sighed Finn.

"It will be freezing in there."

But he could hardly get through the door.

"There you are!" laughed Farmer Finn.

"Perhaps you're not so silly after all."

Put these pictures in the correct order.
Now tell the story in your own words.
Can you think of a different ending?

Puzzle 2

miserable   sad

overjoyed

worried   delighted

happy

Choose the words which best describe Finn at the beginning and the end of the story. Can you think of any more?

Answers

Puzzle 1

The correct order is:

1c, 2f, 3e, 4b, 5a, 6d

Puzzle 2

Beginning   The correct words are miserable, sad.

The incorrect word is overjoyed.

End   The correct words are delighted, happy.

The incorrect word is worried.

Look out for more stories:

For details of all our titles go to: www.franklinwatts.co.uk